Marvelous Me

Library of Congress number pending --

First Edition Second Printing August 2009
ISBN# 978-1-934615-30-0

Written by Dee Ann Culbreath
Illustrations and Cover Art by Denise McMurray
Graphic manipulation and copy editing by Annette Wilcoxson Galloway
Printed and bound in Nashville, Tennessee

Published by Main Street Publishing, Inc.
206 East Main St. Suite 207 Jackson, Tennessee 38301
Toll-free: 1-866-457-7379
Website: www.MarvelousMeBooks.com

Marvelous Me

Written by Dee Ann Culbreath

Illustrated by Denise McMurray

Main Street Publishing, Inc. Jackson, Tennessee

Inspired by Drew
Dedicated to Demetra & Ed

In the morning as I get ready, whom do I see?
Smiling back from the mirror it's Marvelous Me!

At breakfast who helps my mom set out the toast and jam?

Well, Thoughtful Me, of course, because that's part of who I am.

At the bus stop if someone needs a little help, who's there on bended knee?

It's the kind and patient part of myself that I call Courteous Me.

At school when I know the answer,
I want the teacher to see,

That paying attention and studying hard
makes a very Wise Me.

4 × 5 =

At playtime when my friends are choosing teams, they always pick with glee,

The one who gives her very best . . .
"Hooray" for Athletic Me!

It's fun to work with colors and paint birds and bugs and trees,

I love the creative part of myself that I call Artistic Me.

In music class we play our instruments and try to sing on key,

It's great being on stage and sharing with my friends that side called Musical Me.

In the afternoons my friends and I eat cookies and drink our tea,

The part of myself I enjoy the most is the side called Playful Me.

At dinner time I use good manners... I say "thank you," and "ma'am" and "please."

It makes my parents very proud to be dining with Mannerly Me.

After I finish my homework and all of my chores, I'm off to the tub so my parents can see,

That doing what others have asked me to do makes a Responsible Me.

At night I give thanks for all that I am and for the God who made you and made me,

The gifts we've been given and the life we all share makes a Grateful Me.

All of these qualities are inside each one of us, so don't ever forget to see,

That you are helpful and wise and responsible and kind and marvelous . . . just like me!

A Note to Parents . . .

Dee Ann Culbreath, Author

This book is intended to teach children that we are all comprised of many different marvelous qualities. After reading *Marvelous Me* with your child, you might find that the following questions will spark some interesting and enlightening discussions. (They certainly did at my house!)

Name something about yourself that you know is absolutely marvelous.

Can you think of a time when you did something thoughtful for someone at home or at school? How did it make that person feel?

Do you remember when a friend or family member was courteous toward you? What did they do or say?

Name a time that studying hard and paying attention in class taught you something. What did you learn?

What games do you like to play with your friends on the playground or after school? How do you feel after you play or exercise really hard? What good things does exercise do for our bodies?

Have you ever painted or colored a picture? What did the picture look like? What colors did you use?

What is your favorite song? Can you sing it? What instruments do you think it would be fun to play? Do you know anyone who plays those instruments?

What do you and your friends do for fun? Describe a time that you did something really silly.

What are some things that you say when you are using good manners?

Can you remember a time when you did something that was responsible? What did you do? How did it make you feel?

Name three things for which you are grateful. Try to add something to that list everyday!